MW01114191

CLIFFORD'S SCARY HALLOWEEN

by Sonali Fry
Illustrated by Jim Durk

Based on the Scholastic book series
"Clifford The Big Red Dog"
by Norman Bridwell

ISBN 0-439-39453-8

10 9 8 7 6 5 4 3 2

03 04 05 06

Printed in the U.S.A.
First Scholastic printing, August 2002

It was Halloween night. Emily Elizabeth and Clifford were very excited. They were going trick-or-treating!

"Come on, Clifford!" said Emily Elizabeth. "We're going to get so many treats! And you love treats—don't you, boy?"

Woof!

Emily Elizabeth and Clifford met Jetta, Mac, Charley, Vaz, T-Bone, and Cleo outside. Owls were hooting, and the moon was full. Soon they were on their way.

The first house they went to was the Bleakmans'.
Emily Elizabeth knocked on the door. There was no answer.
She knocked again.

"Mr. and Mrs. Bleakman!" yelled Emily Elizabeth.

"Trick or treat!" yelled Charley. Then they heard a loud
creaking sound.

"Maybe the Bleakmans' house is haunted!" said Jetta.

"It's not haunted, Jetta," said Emily Elizabeth. "I'm sure they're home."

Suddenly, the door began to open—very, very slowly—and on the other side were two ghosts!

"Happy Halloween!" yelled the ghosts.

"Run!" yelled Vaz.

Everyone screamed and ran toward the street.

"Wow! They sure tricked us!" said Emily Elizabeth.

"Maybe we'll have better luck at the next house," said Jetta.

"Victor and Pedro's house is close by," said Charley. "Let's go there."

As they walked toward the center of town, bats flew from tree to tree. Cats meowed at the moon. And Clifford stayed right by Emily Elizabeth's side.

The door opened.

"Hello, dearie," said a voice . . . but it wasn't Dr. Dihn.
It was a scary witch!

"Yikes!" yelled Jetta.

Once again, everyone ran.

"It looks like we're not getting any treats tonight!"
said Charley sadly.

"Yeah!" said Jetta. "I'm tired of getting tricked!"

"Let's go back to my house," said Emily Elizabeth.
"Maybe my parents will have a few treats for us."

But when they arrived at the Howards', the yard was filled with witches, ghosts, monsters, and other creepy creatures.

"Surprise!" they yelled.

It was a party—full of Halloween treats!

"We thought it would be fun to trick you this Halloween," said Mr. Bleakman.

"We hope you weren't too scared," said Victor.

"Scared?" said Jetta. "I wasn't scared."
Emily Elizabeth, Charley, and Vaz all looked at Jetta.
"Well . . . maybe just a little bit," she said.

Then it was time for everyone to enjoy their Halloween treats. They bobbed for apples, ate candy, and drank a special Halloween punch.

When the party was over, Emily Elizabeth gave Clifford a big hug.

"The tricks were good," she said. "But the treats were even better!"

Woof!

Clifford agreed!